For Claire, Tom and Maddy with a jungleful of love.

Visit the Anholt's magical bookshop Chimp and Zee, Bookshop by the Sea,
51 Broad Street, Lyme Regis, DT7 3SQ or shop online at www.anholt.co.uk

Chimp and Zee copyright © Frances Lincoln Limited 2001
Text copyright © Laurence Anholt 2001
Illustrations copyright © Catherine Anholt 2001

The right of Laurence Anholt to be identified as the Author
and Catherine Anholt to be identified as the Illustrator
of this work has been asserted by them in accordance
with the Copyright, Designs and Patents Act, 1988.

First published in Great Britain in 2001 by Frances Lincoln Children's Books,
4 Torriano Mews, Torriano Avenue, London NW5 2RZ

www.franceslincoln.com

First paperback edition 2003
This edition published in Great Britain in 2007 and in the USA in 2008

British Library Cataloguing in Publication Data available on request

ISBN 978-1-84507-932-1

Designed by Sarah Massini

Printed in China

1 3 5 7 9 8 6 4 2

Chimp and Zee

CATHERINE AND LAURENCE ANHOLT

FRANCES LINCOLN

This is Chimp. This is Zee.

This is their home in a coconut tree.

Mumkey is hungry, but there are no bananas in the basket. "Which little monkeys have eaten all the bananas?" she says.

Up jumps Chimp.
Up jumps Zee.
"Ha, ha, ha!"
"Hee, hee, hee!"

So Chimp and Zee and Mumkey
go to Jungletown to buy more bananas.

Everyone is busy in Jungletown.

"It is easy to get lost," says Mumkey. "So stay close and don't monkey about."
"Ha, ha, ha!" says Chimp.
"Hee, hee, hee!" says Zee.

Chimp and Zee
think shopping is boring.
They do NOT stay close to Mumkey.
They DO monkey about.

They look for a place to hide.
They find a small grey stone.

"Wherever are those naughty monkeys?" says Mumkey.

Up jumps Chimp.
Up jumps Zee.
"Ha, ha, ha!"
"Hee, hee, hee!"

Chimp and Zee find
a better place to hide –
behind a middle-sized grey stone.

"Wherever are those naughty
monkeys?" says Mumkey.

Up jumps Chimp.
Up jumps Zee.
"Ha, ha, ha!"
"Hee, hee, hee!"

Chimp and Zee find the best hiding place -
inside the banana basket
right on top of the
biggest grey stone of all.

"Ha, ha, ha!"
"Hee, hee, hee!"
"You can't find Chimp."
"You can't find Zee."

Then a remarkable thing happens.

The three grey stones begin to wobble...

The three grey stones begin to shake...

The three grey stones begin to rumble...

Then the three grey stones

get up and...

...slowly walk away.

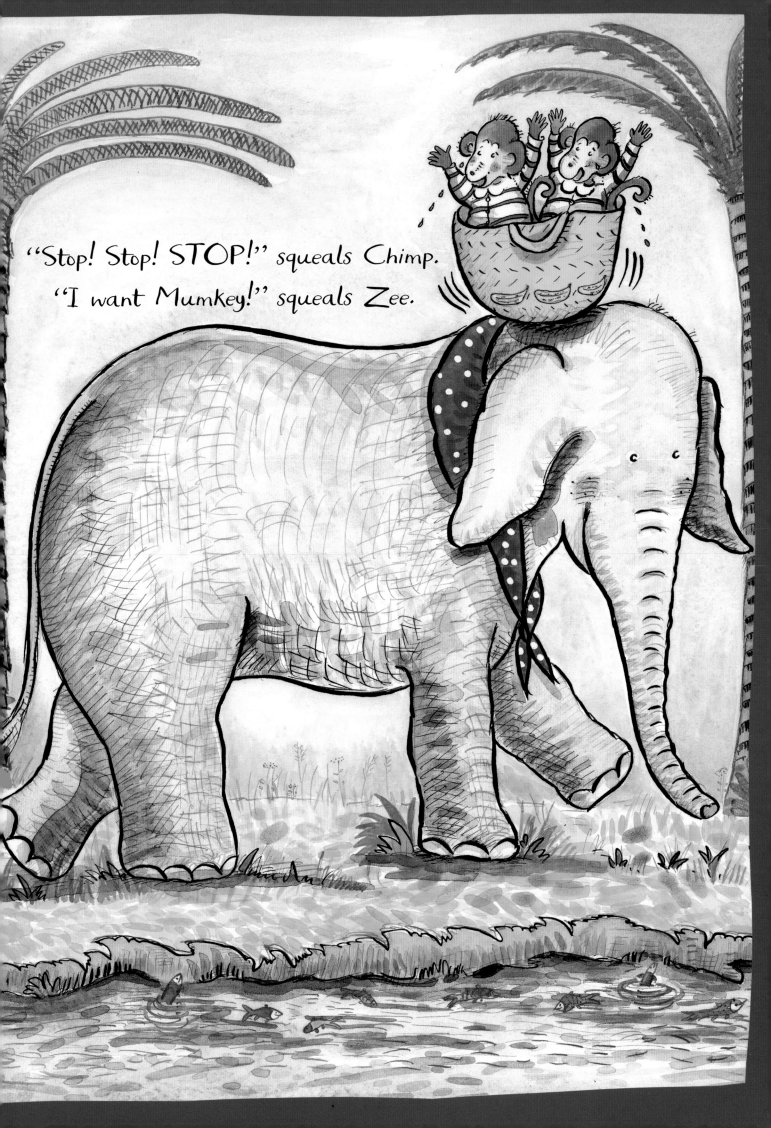

"Stop! Stop! STOP!" squeals Chimp.
"I want Mumkey!" squeals Zee.

Mumkey has finished shopping.

She is ready to go home.

"Wherever is my banana basket?" she says.

"Wherever are those three grey stones?" she says.

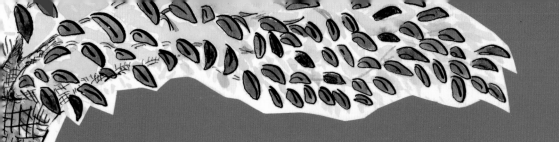

"But most of all - wherever are my little monkeys?" she cries.

And this time, Chimp and Zee do NOT jump up at all.

Mumkey looks high.

Mumkey looks low.

Nobody has seen the banana basket.
Nobody has seen three grey stones.
Nobody has seen two little monkeys.

Everybody is going home.

"Perhaps they have gone back by themselves," says a policeman.

Mumkey goes home as fast as she can. But Chimp and Zee are NOT waiting in the coconut tree. "Deary, deary me! Wherever are Chimp and Zee?"

THIS is where they are - far, far away,
in the deepest, darkest part of Jungletown.
And still the three grey stones keep walking.

The night animals begin to growl - closer, closer, closer.

Chimp and Zee cuddle up together, underneath
the bananas at the very bottom of the banana basket.

Poor little Chimp.
Poor little Zee.
"Boo, hoo, hoo!"
"Wee, wee, weee!"

Then another remarkable thing happens.

The three grey stones are tired...

The three grey stones are thirsty...

The three grey stones go swimming...

The banana basket slips slowly into the river and...

...gently floats away.

"Help! Help! HELP!" shouts Chimp.

"Wee! Wee! WEEE!" shouts Zee.

At home in the coconut tree, Mumkey looks sadly at the empty beds and the moonlit river outside.

Then the most remarkable thing of all happens.

Mumkey sees a basket...

The basket floats closer...

It is full of bananas...

The basket begins to wobble...

Up jumps Chimp.
Up jumps Zee.
"Ha, ha, ha!"
"Hee, hee, hee!"

Chimp and Zee kiss and cuddle and
chitter and chatter and monkey about and…
eat every single banana in the banana basket.

Good night, Chimp.

Good night, Zee.

Fast asleep in the coconut tree.

More CHIMP AND ZEE books
by Catherine and Laurence Anholt
from Frances Lincoln

CHIMP AND ZEE AND THE BIG STORM

It is a stormy day in the coconut tree and Chimp and Zee are
squibbling and squabbling when they get blown away by one big windy whoosh!
Can Mumkey save the day before the troublesome chimps are lost at sea?
ISBN 978-1-84507-069-4

HAPPY BIRTHDAY CHIMP AND ZEE

It's their birthday morning and those mischievous twins are going absolutely bananas –
and so will every child who reads this magical story
and discovers the huge fold-out birthday surprise!
ISBN 978-1-84507-134-9

CHIMP AND ZEE'S WORDS AND PICTURES

Chimp and Zee are back and this time those mischievous twins are going
wild with words and potty with pictures. This wonderful book is crammed with
words to say and play with your own little monkeys.
ISBN 978-1-84507-375-6

Frances Lincoln titles are available from all good bookshops.
You can also buy books and find out more about your favourite titles,
authors and illustrators on our website: www.franceslincoln.com